I0778860

WE

ARE

H.E.R.

WE ARE H.E.R. DEVOTION

Healed, Enough & Reloaded
FOR OUR JOURNEY

KIM HARRELL

ISBN: 978-0-578-78407-6 (Paperback)

 978-0-578-80641-9 (E-book)

Library of Congress Control Number: 9780578784076

Book Cover Design by Tyra J. Harrell

Printed by Prize Publishing House, LLC in the United States of America.

First printing edition 2020.

Prize Publishing House

P.O. Box 9856

Chesapeake, VA 23321

www.PrizePublishingHouse.com

CONTENTS

*AND BLESSED IS SHE WHO BELIEVED THAT THERE WOULD BE A FULFILLMENT OF WHAT WAS SPOKEN TO **H.E.R.** FROM THE LORD.*

-LUKE 1:45

INTRODUCTION

You are in a season of completion - healing completely. God delights in His daughters finishing their assigned journey. God's word will assist in your healing and in believing you are enough. His word purposely gets you reloaded for your purpose here on earth. I am praying this is true for your personal journey, for your relationships, for your next steps, as well as the blooming process of who you are becoming. Through your obedient heart and willing mindset to *Lean Into* the goodness of God, you can finish. Don't you want to have the greatest life ever? If you answered yes, then be done with any excuses or any doubt. Are you up to being the best you? Are you ready to challenge yourself for the next 50 days? Are you prepared for 50 days of consistently coming back to your journal, praying, and putting in the work? You must do the work without quitting and giving up on investing in yourself. Prayerfully, you answered yes.

Below you will find a commitment line for your signature. You are committing to the completion of this journal/devotion by putting the work in each day for 50 days. It's very much like working out in the gym, no sweat-no gain. This is your fresh new season to reap a harvest for you. We are H.E.R. to get results. You will not quit. You will have an accountability partner to check in with.

I give my word that I am **Healing**, I am **Enough,** and I am being **Reloaded** for my journey. I will finish what I started. (because I am H.E.R.)

____

(***Your Signature***)

***As a bonus take a before and after photo *of yourself*. Feel free to post on the JEWLS Facebook page to encourage other women to start the H.E.R. Journey. Go ahead let our H.E.R. Community know you just started the journey with them. ***

MORE ENCOURAGEMENT

Bonus page of ENCOURAGEMENT and your WHY! Never jump right in with this process. Your personal "why" is your press-your motivation for this journey. Take time today to pray, to focus on your life and really spend time with you and what you want for yourself. The journaling and daily inspiration is you investing in self. Your *inner* self.

Are you ready to believe what God has spoken into every part of who you are? In order for you to be H.E.R. (Healed, Enough & Reloaded) for your journey, you have to trust God. This journal is designed for you, a JEWEL that recognizes your life is a journey. These upcoming pages are filled with encouragement to tackle the hard days, good days, painful memories, issues, mistakes, heart breaks, wins, growth, burdens, and just real life. You know why? It's because our journeys are unique but so similar at the same time. We share several things in life that affect us differently but many of us have like experiences.

Visualize a caterpillar transforming into a butterfly-you will transform into a woman with a fresh new perspective of your life, purpose, and the direction that you are headed to.

Though each one of us has a different story we can agree that life does happen, and the more we live it out the more we realize we need encouragement and support daily. Even with the caterpillar, it is totally different from the butterfly. They are not alike at all. It is now time, as you take this challenge and complete your journey, that you will not be the caterpillar anymore. My sister, you will shed your old way of thinking and those patterns of not being enough will no longer exist. Can you repeat this, **"I am transforming even on the days when I don't see or feel it."**?

Each day it is my hope that the reloading will take place. How can you be healed? What can you be healed of? Is healing even real? Does healing exist when for so long you have been broken, left for dead, rejected, abused, neglected, talked down on, raped, divorced, taken for granted, emotionally kicked around and never really understood by people? The answer is located in Luke 1:37, where it speaks to each of us: ***"For with God nothing shall be impossible".*** You are enough. The middle portion of this journal is liberating because once you believe you are healed; you will walk in the healing. As you continue to take steps on your journey, you will step into being enough. Enough what? How am I enough? I have never been enough is probably your next statement. Honey, if you only knew what being fearfully and wonderfully made meant about your "enoughness", the knitting that took place because of your purpose and the way that God knew you before you even hit the womb of your mother. Again, I say, you are enough.

You will get a new supply. You will be filled. You will bloom. You will understand. For this journey, "butterfly", you are being gracefully broken. Reloaded in the sense that for anything that depleted you, you will have an overflow and the purpose on your life will be restocked. The butterfly was once hanging upside down on the twig and had been spinning and spinning...in a protective covering...then the radical transformation happens. See, those spins on your journey are God doing something within you as He still protects you.

As I fired my weapon in the military, when my ammunition that I received to knock down the targets in front of me was gone, I would reload. The reloading for us as women is being filled back up with everything needed to be who we were created to be. You now have a supernatural force and strength that cannot be stopped. What was drained, things that had been taken from you, the mistreatment and even those areas that you were stuck in will no longer hinder you - it moves you differently now. It moves you to come out and keep living. Events in your life had to happen to launch you forward. It was a process. Reloading comes from you agreeing with what God has spoken. You trust that He has already orchestrated a new process for you. **Just for you.**

WHY DID THIS JOURNAL HAVE TO GET INTO YOUR HANDS?

Too much heaviness is in the heart of women that go unhealed. Too many women are emotional wrecks because they honestly believe they are not enough. Friends you have known for years are starting relationships in the midst of being broken. When in fact they do not understand the need to be whole as they start the new relationship. They are seeking to be loved, seeking value, seeking wholeness, when in fact all of this comes from God. It stems from being healed and whole for themselves first. Over and over on our journey we never stop for the reload step. Well, that sums up the why - for us as sisters. We are a community of women who intentionally by faith will be H.E.R. (Healed, Enough & Reloaded) to finish our journeys.

We all will have the birth date and our death date to symbolize the life we lived. But the small dash is the journey. Get in agreement sisters, that our dash will include our healing from God, us realizing that in that time we were always enough, and that God reloaded us to ensure we made a significant impact before that last date. With tears in my eyes, hope in my heart, a burden for broken women and a passion that I cannot shake.... I declare, **WE ARE H.E.R. ON OUR JOURNEY.** God is building us up spiritually to make the dash (of our journey) our best life. God desires for our life here on earth to be abundant. He wants his girls to rock that dash. He wants your dash to represent Him. Come on lets finish our lives in purpose and be fruitful.

WE

ARE

H.E.R.

HEALED, ENOUGH & RELOADED FOR OUR JOURNEY

When Jesus saw

____

(*add your name*) lying there and knew that

____

(*add your name*) had already been there a long time,

he said to ____

(*add your name*), "Do you want to be healed?"

- John 5:6

Day 1

SIT DOWN

There were two sisters. One sister saw Jesus and his Disciples, and she let them in her home. As they were in her home, she continued to be busy with other things within the home. She had a sister who was there with her. Her sister began to listen to Jesus. She felt it was important to spend time with Him and not prepare the meal, reorganize the furniture, or ensure the bathrooms were spic and span. When the sister who opened up her home to Jesus noticed that her sister was inclined to His teaching and not helping her with the busy work, she caught an attitude. One sister was working and prepping things for their visitor. The other sister, on HER journey, knew this was her moment. As a matter of fact, what the other sister saw blew her mind. She looked over with her hands on her hips to see her sister "sit down" at Jesus' feet to listen to His every word. She took the time to get wisdom and teaching that would lead her to the healing she so desperately needed in her life. Can you relate to one of the sisters? Are you so busy that when you welcome Jesus into your home, into your marriage, into your single life, into being a mother, into your business and into your lifestyle you continue to go on with what you are doing and leave Him out? Or as you start this journey you are taking time to listen. You are taking time to sit down at His feet for wisdom, for boldness, for direction, for courage, for instructions, for a push that only Jesus can provide. You have to look into your inner me and say, "What do I need to heal? Why can't I sit down and get what I need?" Your healing matters. Jesus is near you because you let Him in, but you must know that He needs you to spend time with Him daily. Keep coming back to sit down. Choose to put life on pause while He teaches and pours into you daily. While He is there it is your time to get exactly what you need. This time your healing is your personal victory. Shout, "My victory is in my sit down!"

Read Luke 10:38-42 for your H.E.R. Nugget

KEEP POUNDING!!

JOURNAL

1. When you read about Martha and Mary in Luke 10 which sister can you relate to the most?

____

____

____

____

____

____

2. Have you ever invited Jesus into your life and then were too distracted to listen to Him?

____

____

____

____

____

____

3. What will you do daily to sit down, remove distractions, and focus on your Word?

____

____

____

____

____

____

4. Jot down four (4) power words that you will deliberately rely on to start your journey to healing.

____

____

5. Do you desire to be like Mary and spend daily time to take notes and get reloaded for your journey? Yes__ No__

How will you take your first step?

____

____

Day 2

I THOUGHT

I thought...is that something you say to yourself? Is it something that continues to linger in your heart? I thought they would be by my side. I thought someone would be with me through all of my pain. I thought that my best friend would agree with me as I go through this issue. Thinking and having great expectations from others can lead you to disappointments that are not easily shaken out of your mind. If it does not work out for you, how do you feel? Now all of this discussion is when we are hurt or let down by people. Okay, so what about God? As you heal are you expecting God to be with you, to comfort you, and to put you back on your track? I hope you said yes because that is exactly what God wants from you. He wants us to honor Him by realizing He can do the big things that others have dropped. As you heal on this journey, you will have to leave an open area just for God to maneuver. God needs that space in your heart to transform certain things. Are you ready to let go of just your personal dreams so that God can download into you? It is time to rearrange your mind to say, "Let Your will be done God." When you are disappointed on your healing journey, still you have to trust and lean on your new relationship with God. You will not get bitter this time when it does not happen the way you thought. This time open your heart to what God desires for you! In this journey of understanding, you are going to be healed in a way you never imaged because you will accept this is your new healing season. How ready are you to respond to God? Are you ready to release those past disappointments when others did not support you? How will your expectations change now that God is guiding your heart, dreams, vision, and your purpose? During the times of disappointments and times of seeming like you were in a pit, you stopped the healing process. While you were on your way to total healing, things manifested that caused you to quit. Get back on TRACK. You have not made it to a dead end. Take this new route. Many family members could have neglected to show love or support but today have faith that God is still seeing you through. Press into your faith. Press into the fact that your expectation has to be in God so you can win! You have a dream, and you can see yourself healed from so many disappointments in life. That (I thought) is flipped to I Can!

KEEP POUNDING!!

Day 3

MY HEALING SEASON

In the very first book of the Bible, there is a man by the name of Joseph. Joseph had a journey that was preparing him for the life God had already foreknew. Many difficult scenes took place in this one book concerning Joseph (just like in your life) and one was the fact that Joseph had brothers that were jealous of him. Not just jealous but they threw him in a pit and later sold him. This and more happened on Joseph's journey. Years go on and Joseph is in a new place in his life. The place of healing. A place that his family does not know exists. See, when healing takes place others may not recognize quickly. Joseph recognized his brothers, he remembered the hurt, pain, and suffering but he did not respond back to pain with painful words or actions. Joseph forgave them because of his years of being prepared for what God has spoken over his life. Joseph, just like you, had to recognize his season of healing. Grasp the fact that healing is for you. As you heal your words change and your perspective. Changes will take place in how you respond because you can now only speak from a clean and healed heart. You have heard the saying, "Hurt people, hurt people." That doesn't apply to you any longer. On your journey you have to receive the biblical principles and interpret the scriptures to heal your heart - to heal your journey - to guide you on. Yes, your pain has reminded you of how you have been trampled over and the many scenes of your life that have been broken, but God is here to heal. You have a destiny on your life through the pain. You will feel the hurt. This hurt teaches you on your journey. But the hurt won't define your journey. Please grasp the truth that God's word can heal. **Hurt** has caused you to feel the **injuries** on your journey that sex, money, material things, make-up, expensive clothes, another row of heels, alcohol, cigarettes, clapping back, overeating, taking someone else's spouse, and any other "**fillers**" cannot fix, only God can **heal** the injuries and clean your heart. Take time before you move on and invite God into your heart. Let him into the area where it hurts the most. Into the sensitive area of your life. Do not be afraid.

KEEP POUNDING!!

HEALING SESSION:

1.   "Heal me, Lord, and I will be healed." – *Jeremiah 17:14*

2.   He said to her, "Daughter, your faith has healed you. Go in peace and be freed from your suffering." – *Mark 5:34*

3.   "But I will restore you to health and heal your wounds, declares the Lord." – *Jeremiah 30:17*

4.   "Trust in the Lord with all your heart and lean not on your own understanding; in all your ways submit to him, and he will make your paths straight." – *Proverbs 3:5-6*

Today read to feed from these scriptures. Feed where your heart was broken. Feed from the scriptures that you will be restored. Memorize at least one verse that you can hide in your heart.

 The above scriptures are your H.E.R. Nuggets

KEEP POUNDING!!

Day 4

THE WOMAN IN THE MIRROR

Stand in front of the mirror. Hold the mirror in front of your face. This mirror reflects back at you. This mirror should provide a true, up close image of what you look like but not necessarily who you are. This mirror can remind you of the blemish, the wrinkle, the imperfections and, at times, even the glow that you can carry. As you look in the mirror right now, is there anything that you do not like to look at? Is there a breaking point as you look at you? The mirror that you stand in front of each morning is not the same mirror that God looks at when it comes to who He sees. The mirror that you have is important but the mirror that God has is significant because in His mirror, He sees what He created. He sees what He spoke about you. His mirror has compassion for His daughter. God loves you right now as you look at yourself. In the Bible there is a simple but moving scripture that changes the mirror. The scripture paraphrased says that you were made in God's image and that you were designed by God himself. That mirror is everything from your first breath, to your first loose tooth, to your favorite dress, to the day you got your eyebrows arched, to what makes you smile and to every small detail of who you are. God's mirror reflects beauty, a renewed heart, strength from trials, and a purpose that He specifically placed inside of you. You are not just what you view in the mirror. That is what you see with your natural eye. God sees your soul, the heart and just the moment when He said, there would be a YOU. He sees what your heart beats for. He sees everything you won't see for yourself. Take another look. Can you see what God sees? Just look back in the mirror and fall in love with what God says you are. The woman in the mirror has issues but the woman can faith her way out. That woman is you. You are the woman in the mirror, love her.

Read Psalm 139:13-16 for your H.E.R. Nugget

KEEP POUNDING!!

JOURNAL

1. What did you see in the mirror?

____

____

____

____

____

____

2. How will you begin to change your thoughts to the mirror-reflections?

____

____

____

____

____

____

3. What did God say to you concerning His love in this mirror?

____

____

____

____

____

____

4.   Every day, it is important that you answer these questions and lean into what the word is saying to you. You will not go backwards as you heal. Get rid of putting your life in reverse mode. Where are you going?

____

____

____

____

____

____

5.   See a new reflection and purpose. Write it down.

____

____

____

____

____

____

Day 5

YOU GOT HIS ATTENTION

Are you in a place that you want to hear God's voice in your ear? Are you in a desperate situation and you need to hear God call your name? Do you want a turn in your journey? Is this your biggest and greatest fight of all times? God has a word for this fight and for your journey. He is saying to you at this moment...remember His power! The power is in Jesus! The newness is in Jesus. The blind man in the Bible knew that there was power and healing when Jesus came into town. Will you agree with this blind man and agree that whatever you need today, whatever you will need in your journey, it is the power that Jesus brings. You cannot please the crowd and get this power. You have a choice to make. You will not be able to stay quiet and get this power. Do you want to suffer, or do you want to be healed? See, on this journey you have some options. Your strength is in Jesus. Your ability is in Jesus. This is day number 5, 5 represents God's Grace and Favor. He absolutely loves you. You have already turned this way and that way prior and none of it worked. Today is your ***come out on top day***! That is the type of day when it all transforms! As Jesus calls for you, it is because you shouted in His direction. Depression must go. Anxiety must go. Hopelessness must go. The lies of the enemy must go. It did look hard. It was breaking you down. But the Grace of God has taken over. Today open your mouth and know that your calling out to Christ is the reason He stopped. He hears you. Your prayers caught His attention. Your desperate cry changed your situation. Whoever told you that you always want attention-well this is the attention you were looking for. Remember that once the blind man had the attention of Christ, he received his sight. He now could see things on the journey that he couldn't visualize before. When others saw that he could see they began to praise God! Can you jump up and down for your sister who has the attention of Christ? What about you? You can celebrate that you can see now. You have to refuse to be quiet. Get His attention.

Read Mark 10:47-52 for your H.E.R. Nugget

KEEP POUNDING!!

Day 6

WAITING ON MY HEALING PROMISE

Have you ever settled in your pain and just said, "I will be okay. I will just act as if it never hurt me." God has not forgotten your prayer of healing. He has exact timing for you. Hannah went to the altar and prayed so powerfully that the Priest thought she was drunk. It was a prayer with such intensity because it was a pray that launched in her heart. Are you desperate for your healing? People may not interpret your actions properly. The thing is God totally understands. You are going through a season of healing. It is a time of preparation not a time of delays. Do not get those two confused. Though you have silent tears and you have suffered severe pain please remember that God has a promise just for you. The promise will go forth. The promise is your game changer. The promise is tailor made for your journey. Stop looking around at other women and making the mistake of assuming they are moving forward but you are stuck in pain. You have a destiny as you heal in your thoughts. You have purpose that will be fulfilled as you heal. The promise is yours. You can have a miracle. You my sister, will have the promises God has placed inside of you. Hannah cried out to God. God remembered her. She dealt with pain day after day. She was in agony not knowing why it hurt so much. Can you relate to Hannah? Will you trust and lean into the promises of God concerning your healing? Trust that He knows. Lean into great expectation. Will you continue to pray even when it feels like nothing is happening? Nothing can make up for the pain you have lived with. Please note that once you receive your healing promise; ensure to take care of the promise. As Hannah prayed, she also made a promise to God that she would dedicate her child back to Him. And she did. Will you give the healing promise to God and allow him to get the glory out of giving it to you?

Read 1 Samuel 1:9-28 for your H.E.R. Nugget

KEEP POUNDING!!

JOURNAL

1. When do you pray over things that hurt you?

____

____

____

____

____

____

2. How have you demonstrated your desperation for God's answer? Do you call out for attention from others who can't heal you? Do you shut yourself off from others?

____

____

____

____

____

____

3. How can Hannah's story help you in areas where you have not yet produced?

____

____

____

____

____

____

4. Hannah said she was praying out of great anguish. Take time to describe what you have been praying out of? Is it anguish? Is it not having patience? Is it envy of what other women have? Is it anger?

____

____

____

____

____

____

5. Discuss pain. Discuss the wait as you heal. Discuss why it feels lonely as you wait on God's promises. Give one word about Hannah's prayer.

____

____

____

____

____

____

Day 7

NOT DESTROYED

Being you, you have experienced highs and lows in your life. As you become H.E.R. there will be pressure on every side trying to make you turn to camouflaging your true feelings. Sometimes you may even feel like you have been to hell and back as you have vivid flashbacks of pain. Let me express to you, that you will survive. You will stand. You are still here; so, you can still win. You can be troubled on every side but not perplexed. Persecuted but not forsaken. Cast down but not destroyed. Say, "I am NOT DESTROYED." Now believe what you said. This time it's for you. Destroyed means defeated, wipe-out or demolished. You are none of those.

Becoming H.E.R. actually puts you under pressure. Not the type of pressure that explodes but spiritual pressure to expand and stretch you. Expand your thoughts of yourself. Stretch your mindset of how to be healed. Being battered by trouble gives God the opportunity to fight for you. He has not left your side and He will not allow you to be broken without repair. You are coming out of these situations much wiser. You are coming out a better version of you. Explosive in your purpose and empowered to say to yourself, "I will no longer count myself out of the line-up of being H.E.R. I am His Big Idea. Do not reduce your dreams to nothing. At this point of your life, restoration is available. Within you, you have to press in and be determined. The enemy tried to reduce the value of your life by harming you, but God gave His son Jesus for His blood to make these wrongs right, to heal, and to try again. As a matter of fact, roll up your spiritual sleeves and get in position to destroy the devil's swings. Block what matters to you. Protect your heart. Any boxer in the boxing ring tries to redirect the opponents and they keep their guard up. Just remember it's your responsibility to maintain your stance- keep your footing-be stable. Girls Rock, so as soon as you see the enemy in the ring of your journey- come back with the word - (lead hook) will knock his distraction out. You are not destroyed. You just won.

Read 2 Corinthians 4:7-9 for your H.E.R. Nugget

KEEP POUNDING!!

JOURNAL

1. How can the healing that is taking place within you create something special to be used by God? Think of the vessel. How can you be usable as you heal?

____
____
____
____
____
____

2. What is fragile about you that you want God to restore?

____
____
____
____
____
____

3. What do you believe God wants you to carry?

____
____
____
____
____
____

4.   Name the pressures you are experiencing now. Write out the pain that struck you down.

____

____

____

____

____

____

5.   Then write, "I am not crushed, I am healing."

____

____

____

____

____

____

MAKE UP YOUR MIND

Can you take time today to think of yourself as an established woman? An established woman implies that you are firm in your mind as to who you are in God. Set in your mind that you can. God desires you to have a set mind not a mind that wanders off every time there is a roadblock in H.E.R. life. What is taking place right now in your life that is unstable?

____

____

____

____

____

____

As you talk (have your daily discussions) with God are you telling Him what is best for you? Or are you listening to His voice? From here on out we will not allow anything to shift the foundation of our set mind. God has newness for you. You are being built up. MAKE UP YOUR MIND that you will not doubt that God has raised you up above the quicksand and that you can breathe. He is not letting you sink. The walls, the obstacles are being torn down. However, what you think of yourself is what you will be. Repeat this: **"I am what I think I am. I will be what I say I am. I affirm myself with words that Christ says about me."** Surrender your old way of thinking, so your healing can be contagious, spreading from your brain, to your eyes, to your ears, to your heart, to your voice, to your attitude, to your future, and to every part of the new you. Catch on fire with possibilities. Illuminate. Shine. Do not dim down. God is no longer negotiating with you; it's done. This all takes having a made-up mind. You have a decision to make. Don't change your mind concerning you. Your undivided attention is required. Clear out the clutter. It is your job to keep your mind focused. You have to pour into your own thoughts.

Read Colossians 3:2 for your H.E.R. Nugget

KEEP POUNDING!!

JOURNAL

1. What does SETTING your mind mean to you?

____

____

____

____

____

____

2. During healing what will you focus on? List things that will assist you.

____

____

____

____

____

____

3. Do you trust that a positive mindset can lead you to true healing? How?

____

____

____

____

____

Day 9

BREAKING POINT

Why haven't you invited some backup into the pain that you have been experiencing? The backup is God taking up for you. God is your strong tower. When you are the daughter of the King, you have to see yourself wearing a crown. Allow the healing to "break in" - breaking in means even if you do not want it; it still happens. This type of breaking in will corner your inward feeling and allow you to surrender it over. Right now, as you read are you feeling half put together? Are you going day to day bearing the hurt but trying to move on anyway? Today, make this your last day of being locked up without the bail. Jesus paid for you to be released and healed. You can be free from this pain. Get in a place where you can pray. A place where you can talk to God. If that place is your room, your bathroom, your closet, or just an area where you can just share with GOD....it's a good place. He has been awaiting your arrival. You have carried too much weight, heaviness, and stress. No matter what you face, right now is the time to say boldly, **"Oh that's the end of me taking any and everything. I have a promise. My life will align with the word of God."**

You were down; but you are not knocked out. No longer will you just sit on the sofa of self-pity. God kept you for a purpose. You are so valuable. Do not blame the enemy. You must be vocal; let your voice be heard. Open your own mouth and let God know you are still all that He created you to be. Tell Him you need His STRENGTH. Confess to Him you will take AUTHORITY back. This is your BREAKING POINT. No more carrying the pressure. No more anxiety. No more laying it down and picking it back up. No more pulling the Band-Aid back to pick with it. Uncover it to God and let it heal this time. No more waiting to be next. It's your turn to be H.E.R.! Declare and believe you're healed.

Read Ephesians 4:27 for your H.E.R. Nugget

KEEP POUNDING!!

JOURNAL

1. Look up the word authority and write the definition below:

____

____

____

____

____

____

2. Explain for your life what it means not to give the enemy authority and opportunities over your life.

____

____

____

____

____

____

3. What ways have you previously allowed the enemy to rule in your life?

____

____

____

____

____

4. Taking back all authority in your life is a part of your healing journey. Find one way to thank God.

____

____

____

____

____

____

5. Write your own words of commanding yourself to be strong when it comes to your future.

____

____

____

____

____

____

Day 10

SHIFTING TO SHAPING

As you lean into your new beginning things will seem to be moving around. Pieces of your life will seem to be out of place. Life has to SHIFT as you become H.E.R. Your mindset towards who you are is SHIFTING in a new direction. This shift is spiritual. It's not overnight. Some pain that has been a part of you for years will have to be surfaced up once again. There will be times where you wish that it weren't happening. You're going in the direction where the road is not a dead end this time. A direction where you don't have to make a U-turn. If you keep going and push through this process, you will have traveled to a place of peace. A place where you know you deserve to be. You are going into a healthy place. You have a word inside of your heart now that is rooted. This word can't be yanked away because of let downs, bad news, circumstances, news reports, lies told on you, not being selected, people walking out of your life, past mistakes, and not even by your own doubts. This is a good place to declare, "Lord, help my unbelief."

This shift pushes you to grow. Recognize that as the shifting takes place God is working inside. Don't run from this uncomfortable position. You are God's masterpiece and as He shifts, He never throws you off the wheel. He only pinches away until He forms something out of you that can be used. MOLD H.E.R. SHAPE H.E.R. RELOAD H.E.R.

Good news! The shifting removes what once held you down, held you back and kept you motionless in your purpose. Where is your highlighter? Highlight this: I am SHAPED in a unique way by God. He made me useful. I will be used by God. What I do not need to carry any longer, He will remove. What I needed but did not have, He will provide. I believe this for my journey.

Read Jeremiah 18:1-12 for your H.E.R Nugget

KEEP POUNDING!!

JOURNAL

Verse 4 states, "But the (pot) he was SHAPING from the clay was marred in (his) hands; so, the potter formed it into another pot, shaping it as seemed best to him."

1. You are the pot when it comes to being healed. As you think of the marred clay, how have you been marred?

____

____

____

____

____

____

2. If you received God's shaping in your life what would it involve from your perspective?

____

____

____

____

____

3. Are you ready to surrender to God's shaping and molding? _______________ The process of pinching the past away hurts but the healing will be a process that brings great joy. What does joy look like for you?

____

____

____

____

____

____

You have to take your position on the potter's wheel. It's your turn. Are you ready to go down to the Potter (God) on bended knee? Yes, pray to God for the shaping.

**If you are a part of a women's small group or book club, discuss shifting and shaping. Take time to pray for other women who are ready to be healed in areas and shaped for their H.E.R. journey. **

Jot down some of the responses:

____

____

____

____

____

____

____

____

Day 11

INFLUENCE

Why can't you believe that you are stronger now? She girds herself with strength, she can be trusted......who can find a virtuous woman? This woman is living with standards, has integrity, and most importantly is willing to be disciplined. How many undisciplined people are you surrounded by? H.E.R. is not easy to be. Your life will have to go through some heartache and pain topped off with difficult situations, but you must open your mouth again and declare, **"My God is not slow to fulfill the promises as others may think, but He is so patient toward me, He doesn't wish that I should perish, but that I should reach repentance."** (2 Peter 3:9) You have repent to God when you know He is not pleased. Be willing to spend time in prayer and get the necessary character needed to go forward. As a Proverbs 31:10 woman, you are worth more than jewels. You are so important to your family, your circle, and God.

You have INFLUENCE. God thought of you strategically. You are different. You are unique. You are becoming. Speak well of yourself, Sis. Hard hearts won't allow the love of Christ to flow in. Will you be the woman of influence? You have to first believe that you have the capacity to empower other women. Before you can begin to walk in that influence, you must be truly healed. Say this, **"Lord, I love you. I know it is time for more in my life. Heal my thoughts. Heal me so I can share my healing testimony to whom you guide me to. The influence I desire to have will come from a humble place in my heart. My influence will be healthy and life changing."** There is a story in Luke chapter 7, of a woman with an alabaster jar. The jar contained expensive perfume. She was referred to as sinful. She broke the jar, poured the contents on the head of Jesus. If you are ready to influence be prepared to "pour", kneel and have faith. The alabaster jar was her heart. Influencing also takes giving what is in your heart to God. He told her and he is telling you, you are forgiven. Now go forth.

Read Titus 2:7 for your H.E.R. Nugget

KEEP POUNDING!!

JOURNAL

1.   As you learn the scriptures, you also have to apply them to your lifestyle. This is a point where you must read the word of God to feed from it. Get nourishment from how the word speaks to your heart and your life.

____

____

____

____

____

2.   Many women do not understand how important it is to choose the right mentor. Whose voice are you listening to? Ensure you trust their instructions as they guide and lead you. Pray concerning seeking a mentor, leadership, and development.

____

____

____

____

____

3.   Are you ready to pour your heart out to God?

____

____

____

____

____

Day 12

DON'T SETTLE

Many, many, many times in life we tend to take the good. We snatch what we think is good. Oh, that is good for me! That will work out good for my life. The truth is God wants to give you more. He has more than good for his daughters. God has more than enough. The Lord has the destiny, the provision, the security, the answers, the perfect will and what He asks is for you to wait. It can be destructive for your entire life if you continue to move ahead and settle for good when there is absolutely GREATER. You are becoming all that Christ created you to be. In this transformation you must let go of good enough. Favor that is insane awaits you. Doors opened wide await you. Things you never asked for is waiting for you. Positions that you are not qualified for is waiting for you. God is your source. Let Him do the far-out things for you. He has extra in store if you will not settle. How many times have you settled for less? How many times did you dummy down to settle for others to get what was meant for you? You don't have to have things in your life watered down. Let God provide more than you ever expected. God will bring promises to you that earlier seemed like it could never happen. It can happen! God will come through for you! When you settle for just good are you demonstrating that you don't trust God with His PROMISES? Trust God for His blessings. Trust God with your life. He knows what is best for every single part of your life. Give God the whole pie, not a slice. Strive for Better! Do not ignore when you know God is speaking to your heart about what He has for you. When you are a daughter of God, you can hear His voice over doubt. So, trust that when it comes to the plans God has for you, it is settled. Agree with those plans.

Read Genesis 16:2 for your H.E.R. Nugget

KEEP POUNDING!!

JOURNAL

1. What are some of the promises that you are waiting for?

____

____

____

____

____

____

2. What did Abram do as you read Genesis 16:2?

____

____

____

____

____

____

3. Sarah asked her husband to sleep with the maidservant to have a child because she didn't want to wait for GREAT, she settled for her desires. What have you settled for on your journey that you know today was not what God wanted?

____

____

____

____

____

____

The promise was for Sarah to have the child not the maidservant

Do not birth Ishmaels instead of waiting for your Isaac.

Study this scripture and know the promise is Enough.

Journal what you received:

____

____

____

____

____

____

____

____

____

Day 13

REFINED

Preparation mode is significant. God moves at His time. This is called your REFINING season. Think of it as your personal, spiritual Autumn for your soul. Doubt is falling off of you. Negative comments are dropping out of your mind. As you wrap your heart around "I'm Enough", that's when you will sense refining. Refining means God is making small but specific changes in you. God wants you to succeed. You need adjustments in your heart that only He can do. Are you willing to accept character development? God has closed doors and you still tug on the locks. Let it stay shut. Are you allowing God to mold you into H.E.R.? No longer can bitterness live within. Don't allow bitterness to build a foundation. No more patterns. No more cycles. This behavior only hurts. Now is the time to have the "want to" attitude. Let's get the renovation done. You will no longer be a critical woman. You are releasing this now; it's a choice you have to make. It's time for you to get on your knees and worship God. Thank Him and praise Him all day long? Remember God will not let pain happen without him placing something new inside of you. Refining brings forth your new life. Anger can't refine. Getting back at folks will not shape purpose. God is our vindicator. Accept that right now. You want your life back, right? You want your peace back? You want to go forward? Keep your heart right and clean so your prayers can be answered. God is ready to do greater for you. God wants you to learn through this cleansing process. This process is your detox. It is not going to be easy becoming H.E.R. There will be delays you will not like; but it's all necessary. Every single thing you went through, whether it was painful or not, teaches you for your next assignment. Do not continue to let things stress you out. Refining is getting that unwanted nasty behavior and stubbornness off of you and out of you. Those spiritual leaves are falling all around you. Can you see yourself diving into the leaves and dancing in the pile? It is off of you! Are ready for the new season of fulfillment and growth? Enjoy the shedding. Long for the change. Look forward to the old being bagged up and taken away. Use your own spiritual rake and gather the pile to be burned. The refining is necessary. The refining is a process. The refining clears a new way for your continued journey.

Read 1 Peter 4:12 for your H.E.R. Nugget

KEEP POUNDING!!

Day 14

GET UP

No more sugarcoating life experiences. Your journey has had difficult and unpleasant moments. Sugarcoat means that we try to make things sweet or better than it is. Things, people, and some dreams have died. Some relationships, friendships, leaderships, memberships, fellowships, and hardships have sunk. You were wondering why it hurt, why they left, why it didn't work out and why they let you down. To be honest, anger has taken over because of wasted time; time that won't return. Focus on this: The Get Up! Wipe those tears, get out of feelings, and come down from the emotional roller coaster. No longer will dysfunction rule but you will be functional and productive. Launch your best life! You have decided to live! Get up from that place of anxiety. Get up from that place of rejection. Get up from negative thinking of yourself. Get up from embarrassment. Get up from looking stupid. Get up from why me. Get up from I am not enough. Get up from I can't move on. Get up from everyone is laughing at me. Get up from crazy thoughts. Get up from my life doesn't matter. Get up from I'm not married yet and I'm over 40. Get up from I never get the good opportunities. Get up from my father was nowhere to be found. Get up from he cheated. Get up from I knew he cheated and took him back again. Get up from I made the wrong choices. Get up from blaming others. Get up from you can't start over. Get up from your pity party. Jesus told the man to GET UP, pick up his mat, and move from that place. He had been in a place for 38 years. What is your place? Some conditions will hinder you if you stay down in it. This is you call to action. Don't you dare go back and stretch out on that mat. Excuses will not work.

You must believe that after you have gotten up and moved, that God is well able to build again. You can be restored. You can move forward. Surround yourself with positive ladies. Get on up! Get up! Ask God to continue to command your path.

Read John 5:8 for your H.E.R. Nugget

KEEP POUNDING!!

JOURNAL

Begin your handwritten request to God and talk to Him about the areas you will be getting up from. Explain to Him the baggage that kept you there. Then, in your own words express how you are enough.

____

____

____

____

____

____

____

____

____

____

____

____

____

____

____

____

____

Sign _______________________________ (I am Enough)

Signed by me.

Day 15

GO THROUGH IT

Why does going through hardship carry so much pain and anxiety? Things happen that women do not want to admit to. Question: What is it about yourself that you would like to be transformed? Is there a certain condition you want to disappear? How about your spiritual life? As you go through certain parts of your life will be different; that's what transformation means. Open your spiritual eyes to get to know God even the more, focus on Him. God is love, patience, compassion, generous, and forgiving. What do you see in yourself that is like Him? God told you that you were made in His image. The H.E.R. journey begins in a place of separation. Things that God will do inside of you will be private. The Samaritan woman better known as the woman at the well, was spiritually transformed. He takes time to spend just with you. God has called you away from certain people, places, habits, and familiarity so that you can go THROUGH IT with Him. God has been shielding you and the Bible speaks to you by saying that God is your strong tower. Let Him be your hiding place as you go through it. Going through moves you closer to him and further from yourself. He makes sure that you are fully loaded to continue this intentional journey. You are blooming. You are growing up. You are seeing clearly. You are not in your feelings. You are better. You are not holding back anymore. You are not crazy. You are not losing it. You are being shaped into all that God wants you to be. It is elevation time! It is H.E.R. time. Get locked in..... you are ENOUGH. This spiritual enough is not ordinary. You are finally seeing what God saw as He created you. (smile) I see you Sis! You have the right to smile because being enough looks super good on you. That woman at the well looked the same as she went back into town and shared her transforming experience. What they couldn't see was how full of joy her heart was and they didn't notice her empty hands. No longer did she carry the jug for the water. Now she carried a sense of who she really was. Keep going through and get what you have always wanted. Only you know what you want.

Read Romans 12:12 and John 16:33 for your H.E.R. Nugget

KEEP POUNDING!!

JOURNAL

1. When you read that Christ has overcome the world, what are your thoughts?

____

____

____

____

____

____

2. How does having peace in Him allow you to enjoy being enough? Because with His peace you are His....

____

____

____

____

____

____

3. If you could help someone else when it comes to them being enough, what words would you use?

____

____

____

____

____

____

4. Is there a scripture you could share? Write it here:

____

____

____

____

____

____

5. Share your scripture with a friend today.

____

____

____

____

____

____

Day 16

STEP INTO IT

There are going to be moments on your H.E.R. journey that you will not be able to see that you are called for roles other than those you have been serving in. You may even feel unqualified to launch out to the tug of greatness. The tug is God propelling you to other areas. The results are in, He is 99.5 % your Father. When God is your Father it is important to trust that He has equipped you to be a winner. There is a special gift and anointing that you have not begun to walk in. The fear in you must die. What do you have to let go of so you can pick up who God says you are? Your very own thoughts are holding you down. Sis, you are becoming more of who God has called you to be but that is not where your mind is. Align your mind. You can't be who you want to be and who God has planned for you to be simultaneously. Our God is not using your new journey to ruin your life. God is putting the pieces of your life together in a manner that builds your destiny. Focus, study, pray, intentional, and on purpose are action words that will push you closer to what God has. Step into it! Step into that new circle, step into that power squad, step into that new mindset, step into that new career, step into that promise that has always been yours. You knew there was a pulling, but you just couldn't articulate it. I don't know what you had to remove or release to get to this place of your journey but wipe your face. This is a God move. You are still blooming. You still have access. You still have the ability. You assumed you needed that man, that friend, that money, that connection to step into it but God is talking to you right now. His one word can do more than that person giving you the hook up could ever do. God wants you to be thirsty for Him. Are you still thirsty to stay on this track? Are you thirsty enough to know you are not validated by people? Are you thirsty for God to show you your true value? Because you stepped into it you have new boldness and fresh confidence! Lay hold of that part of your life, that fear took all these years. Get what belongs to you by fixing your mind on God. Step into that thirst and be quenched! Your spirit has been revived!

Read Judges 15:18-19 (Message Bible) for your H.E.R. Nugget

KEEP POUNDING!!

Day 17

MOVING THRU H.E.R.

Begin to expect manifestation of the supernatural in your own life. You have to look forward to it. Things are going to be displayed and seen in your life. Right now, imagine things happening just for you. See God stepping in for you. Hold on to the promises that God will never leave you nor forsake you. You have to begin to hear the word of God and speak the word over and over until it becomes a part of your heart. Please receive the word; grasp the word and Sis, work the word. The word is for you. Ask God daily, what is my purpose for this day? Let God know you are seeking Him, and you want your heart to beat for Him. You want each molecule and cell and organ to all function and move as one for Him. This may all sound crazy, insane, and ridiculous, but abiding in God looks different. Are you expecting amazing things for your life? You have a decision to take what God is providing for you. Will you choose the overflow that GOD has sprung forth for you? This is personal. You have to take the teaching and realize you have strength now. Your relationship with God should illuminate your entire being. Are you hungry daily to please God? Does He see you depending on and pressing in for Him? GOD CAN USE YOU as you commit to trusting Him with your life.

Are you putting on the thoughts of God? Are you letting down your own will for His will? This means are you wanting what God wants for you? You won't see everything today but keep sticking closer to God and desire to be in HIS presence. When you examine your relationship with God, are you satisfied with what you experience being near Him? How can you make it stronger? How can you build your life? How can you share this blueprint with the world? Sis, when you love God, you do His will. You have to allow God to be your source. Let God in. This is spiritual. This is not the natural way of thinking; it's growing time. When God begins to move through you; imagine a tie-dye t-shirt. As you tie your shirt, you dip it into the different color dyes. No longer is this t-shirt one plain color, it has taken on the colors that you allowed to soak in it. What God is doing through you is going to change you. It will be a part of your life. His thoughts become yours. The colors, the creativity, the transformation in your heart will flow to every path of your journey. Cast your way of thinking out into the deep where God is there waiting to show you a new way and "His way" of doing things. Expect your nets (business, ministry, goals, dreams, desires, brands, and relationships) to be EXPANDED and expect to prosper so much you want to share with others. You are ENOUGH.

Read 1 Corinthians 2:1-5 and Matthew 5:6 for your H.E.R. Nugget

KEEP POUNDING!!

JOURNAL

1. Journal here how you are enough? Create confidence in yourself.

____
____
____
____
____
____

2. Write what these scriptures are saying to your situation today?

____
____
____
____
____
____

Day 18

AT THE BOTTOM OF THE BARREL

There will be times in your life that you will not be selected. Folks may not look at you the way God does. They may blow you off or do not see you as a gift. The same people think that you are not enough. In our Bible, David was not chosen. In fact, when all the brothers were called to the line-up, it's as if David was not significant. But who have you decided to be? But who have you decided to follow? Something is shifting for you. It's your decision to walk out your purpose even when they did not pick you. The good news for your day is that God is saying you are the one. You are the one that He has plans for and a purpose to fulfil. You are ENOUGH. You are not at the bottom of the barrel. Lift your head back up. People are waiting on your gift. God wants you to start dreaming one more time. You are necessary and God wants to use you to light up the place. Whether others see you in the back doing the hard work or whether they know you have already been selected or not. You make your own declaration. During this time Jesse has eight sons and he did not see the purpose or plan in his very own son. Yes, David was left out. Do your ever feel left out? Do you have friends who always bring up what you used to do? David had killed not only a bear but also a lion. You too have done great things. You have helped in the background and no one ever saw your value. Listen to me, though David wasn't picked by his family, he was picked out of the barrel by God.

Read 1 Samuel 16:11-12 for your H.E.R. Nugget

KEEP POUNDING!!

JOURNAL

1. Have you ever compared your gift to the gift of another woman?

____

____

____

____

____

____

2. How did you feel when you were not selected when you thought you should have been?

____

____

____

____

____

____

3. God wants to use you to do something new. God is going to use what is in you to bless what is still around you. Begin to write what God has in your heart right now.

____

____

____

____

____

____

4. Have you ever devalued what God has placed inside of you?

____

____

____

____

____

____

This is a prayer for you today: Lord help my sister flow with what You have put inside of her. Never, ever, ever, allow her to compare herself or devalue her gift. Lord keep her. Lord direct her journey and let her stay on track. Lord speak to her heart today so she will accept that she is enough. Lord she is amazing and let her realize she has been chosen and selected for Your perfect plan in Your perfect time. God do not take Your hands off of her life. This is my prayer. Amen.

Day 19

H.E.R. PRAYER DAY

Lord, You are perfect in all Your ways. You are my Lord. You are H.E.R. everything. I ask You to forgive me of my sins. Create in me a clean heart as I speak to You. You said You would never leave me and great is Your faithfulness. You are my help in the time of trouble on my H.E.R. journey. I can't do life without You. I am really trying. You are my God. You are the only true and living God. There is nobody like You. You know everything about me. You created me. You are my way maker and my healer. I trust You. I exalt You and bless You at all times. I lean on You. Your name is above every name and I honor You. You are mighty. Wonderful is Your name. You are my Father. You are amazing. You are worthy of my praise. You always come through for me. You are able. You are capable. You are my strong tower. You are holy. You deserve my praise. I give You honor. Your word is true concerning my life. All that You have for me will come to pass. The gift you gave me will make room for me. I believe that for my life. I tuck that in my heart. Thank you for listening and responding. Thank you for doing what needs to be done within me. Heal my thoughts. Heal my heart. I want to be whole again. I know You hear me right now and You are moving in my situation. You are blessing me right now. Thank You for never lying to me. Thank You for equipping me. Thank You for supporting me and thank You for stabilizing me. Today I want to move with You. Today and always I want my journey to be led by You and blessed by You. Today I want to lean and depend on You. I Love You Daddy. Take full control. This time I won't quit on me. I throw myself at your feet. I want this victory. Thank you. Thank you. It's me God, on my journey with my sisters - bless us. Amen.

KEEP POUNDING!!

Day 20

BUILD NOW

The Lord is calling H.E.R. to BUILD NOW! Do you know it's time for you to toil and to work so you will always have? Don't stop pushing. Get in a position to be restored so that you can be focused. A focused position is a determined position. You have a great work to complete. Do not come down from your new prayer life. Do not come down from your new boldness. Do not come down from your next level in God. You must build. Building is not an easy task, but you are equipped for this movement. There is no time to procrastinate in this season. Can't you see yourself starting? Can't you see yourself finishing strong? Get ready! Keep working! Do not waste time anymore. It's time to work with what you have, Sis. Work your vision NOW. Don't come down from your good work. Distractions come in all forms to get you to stop building, to stop setting goals, and to stop you from dreaming; don't take the bait. In Nehemiah chapter 6, it was stated, "I knew they were scheming to hurt me." Go ahead and send the message, "I can't come down from my great work. I can't stop building my legacy. I can't stop building because the work can't come to a standstill." This is a good place for you to read Nehemiah and it is the perfect time to ask the Lord for strength. Your purpose will be completed, your assignment is vital, your vision will be fulfilled, your dreams will come true and your gift will make room for you. Are you ready to move forward? It is building time for you, which signifies you are putting something together that matters. Put it together! Start assembling! Set it up! Build on! Set up camp! Add on to what you have started! Extend it for expansion! The space shall be filled - brick up!

Read Nehemiah 6 for your H.E.R. Nugget

KEEP POUNDING!!

Day 21

THE MAIN THING

God wants you to accept Him as your Lord and head of your life. Make Him the center above the issue, the separation, the stress, the wealth, and all the situations. Will you accept Christ today? That means do you want to spend time in His word and allow His word to govern your heart? That means that you accept Him in your Heart, and you believe He gave His life for you. God wants you to walk in righteousness and to be a light in this world. That means He wants you to shine because His word guides your words, your thoughts, and your lifestyle. You will have a different walk and be renewed. God wants you to worship Him. Will you give God praise with the fruit of your lips? That means to express to God that you love Him and trust Him by just expressing it through your words. You were created to worship God. God wants you to be praying, this is your way to communicate with Him. Talk with HIM. Chat with HIM. Receive from HIM. The Bible says to pray without ceasing; don't stop. God wants you to hear and listen to His words. Faith comes by hearing His word. Hearing the word of God means to meditate on His word, to study, and to be in fellowship with other believers/small groups. God wants you to be a DISCIPLE.

This is a personal follower of Him. One who is a lifetime learner of Christ and represents Him. This represents your relationship with Him. We can't be stable if we do not get His word. If you do not receive anything else from this devotion, the MAIN THING is for you to establish a relationship with Christ. No more following rules and trying to do everything right. It's H.E.R. time. It's time for you to be saved. This is the journey of being Healed, Enough & Reloaded because you are embracing Jesus and you are making an effort to abide (staying close and zooming in) to be pleasing to God. This is one of the most important decisions of your life! It's confessing with your mouth and heart that Jesus is real in your heart! So many women are lost, broken, and need a breakthrough. God will use YOU to build H.E.R. back up. You are important to H.E.R. comeback. We have to pull our sisterhood on the Lord's side. Will you be commissioned today to go forth and reach? We will not sit back anymore; you are an agent of change! If you already know the Lord, then continue to share His Good News! Matthew 6:33 tells us to seek the Kingdom of God and His righteousness first. Sis, we have a responsibility to make Christ first. Continue to ignite within so there can be an outburst (an expansion) of winning souls in the H.E.R. community! Just like God raised up Moses to lead and to reach people, he wants to use YOU now. Who can you share with today? Jot down a few names____

Let's pray for H.E.R. heart now. "Lord we love You. We know in this season it's time for us to reach our sisters. God give me words and a heart to share with H.E.R.? I know I am chosen by You, according to John 15:16, for a time such as this. I want to share. I need Your boldness because I have a special assignment to win sisters to your Kingdom. Go before me and soften hearts. I am building for your glory. Amen."

KEEP POUNDING!!

Day 22

NOTHING ORDINARY ABOUT ME

You are marked for so much more! God has a special purpose tailored for you. Just you. Didn't those power words encourage you? You will no longer believe that you are just a face in the place. Confess this in your heart: **"I am not ordinary. God has a platform that my gift will illuminate, for His glory."** If you never thought that God would blow your mind; rethink that. Take a glimpse at the life of Esther. In chapter two of Esther (which means star) around the ninth verse it states that she had favor. Not only did she have a lovely figure, but she was beautiful. Point out the beauty of yourself. It's all of you. You have true beauty inside of you. God puts special things within you to bring something beautiful on the outside as well. You are long overdue. How long has it been since you jiggled your arms in the mirror and pulled up your shirt and squeezed your gorgeous tummy? It's the beauty of being you. Take more time to look at YOU in the mirror and admire true beauty. The purpose of your life is great. Esther was chosen to bring salvation to God's people. She was not and you are not

ORDINARY. But the situation she went through was not a joy ride or pleasant. Neither will yours. Things are about to start changing for you. Esther had beauty treatments for one whole year in preparation for her assignment. She had to follow strict instructions. She had to trust God. She had to be courageous. How can you prepare? How can you start getting ready for your "next"? She became Queen and had favor with the King. Esther was crowned. Sis, today you are wearing the crown. The favor of God has found your current location on your journey. It's H.E.R. time and you are H.E.R. Take this season of preparation and listen closely to what God has for you. You are not ordinary; you are very valuable and special.

Read Esther 2 for your H.E.R. Nugget

KEEP POUNDING!!

Day 23

THAT'S INSANE

The definition of insanity is doing the same thing but expecting a different result. Pastor Mike Jr. (Rock City Church) said it this way, "Insanity is making moves that make no sense to man but perfect sense to God." What can you do with your insanity today? Every move you make nor every dream you have will make sense to others and you shouldn't expect it to. What you have in you can't be shared with everyone. You also won't be able to do things your way. Your way brings your results. God doesn't think like your friends. God doesn't think like you. He begins to download vision in you that everyone can't handle. Its far beyond what we can imagine! People will leave you because of your insanity day, your insanity month, and your insanity lifestyle. When God moves in an insane way it's unbelievable! Don't be bothered by this. Don't try to figure it out. There are so many areas in your life that you need to be INSANE about. That means you are taking it to another level, and you are doing it in excellence. It's like you hearing from God and just saying I know He knows the plans He has for me and they are for me to prosper and to succeed. Being H.E.R. already requires a bit of this insane thinking. Insane healing. Insane Enough. Insane Reloading. Let's not stop there. Okay, now write down areas in your life and/or your relationship with Christ that you now can see where INSANITY has to kick in. I am believing God for

INSANE____.

INSANE____.

INSANE____.

INSANE____.

INSANE____.

Read 1 Corinthians 2:9 for your H.E.R. Nugget

KEEP POUNDING!!

Day 24

FOCUS ANYWAY

You have a purpose. Your purpose must have your FOCUS. The Shunammite woman focused on making a resting place for Elisha the prophet. She insisted that Elisha would stop and have a meal when he was in town. She knew what her purpose was in that season. She never lost focus on making life easy for someone else. She did not have a child at the time. This woman like you and I had a certain purpose in a certain season of her journey. As life continued on her journey, Elisha remembered how this woman focused anyway. Elisha wanted to bless her. He asked her what she needed. She replied, "Life is good, and I am secure with what I have." Are you able to say today, that you are secure-with what you have? Even though you may have unanswered prayers will you focus anyway? See when the Shunammite woman kept her focus and served her purpose she was given a promise. The promise was she would have a son that same time the next year. She had a son as promised. Do not allow distractions to keep you from the blessing. Had this woman sat around in her feelings, she may not have gotten the desire that was in her heart as she served. Get focused. Stay focused. When no one supports you, stay focused anyway. When it seems God has not answered, focus anyway. When the people you thought would understand and they don't--focus anyway. You are focused on what God has for you! If you are going to be H.E.R. you must know what the word of God says about your life and your future. You have to know that with Christ guiding you; you can walk in your purpose no matter how hard it seems. Go forward as you focus on birthing your dream and your vision. You have confidence. You have strength. You have wisdom. You are anointed for this. You are BOLD. You will not hold on to brokenness. A message was in her story and there is a message in your story. You must be secure in God's will. You are enough! You have a RELOADED life, heart, and soul.

Read 2 Kings 4 for your H.E.R. Nugget

KEEP POUNDING!!

<h1 style="text-align:center">Day 25</h1>

—ᴧ—

IT WAS NEVER FOR YOU

Have you heard of the woman with the issue of blood in the Bible? This woman had a serious issue. Have you ever experienced an issue? I mean an issue that took over your life. You wake up and it's still there. You hang out with friends and the issue won't get lost in traffic. You thought it was just something you had to go through for yourself. The issue of blood was never just for the woman in the Bible. That issue was for you. Had she not had faith we may have never heard of her issue. Does this take the pain from your issues? No. It did hurt your heart. But every painful experience is not yours. Listen, to me. It was never for you. God chose to use you so that you could build H.E.R. up. This affliction was purposely there so you could help your sister. **It was never for you.** The affliction, the abuse, the suffering, the lies, the affair, the debt, the frustration, the neglect, THE ISSUE, the forced abortion, the foreclosure, the repo of the car, the separation, the child not talking to you, the stepfather touching you, the mother (who didn't believe you) and stayed with him when you told

88

the truth, being on the 5th floor for mental evaluation, and the losing of everything was all wrapped in the Grace of God. He already knew that He would never give you more than you could bear. You still don't understand it, but His ways are not your ways and we definitely do not have it figured out the way God does. I know you're asking, why did all this have to happen to ME? Why did it have to hurt so much? Only God has all the answers for you. This is one of the reasons sisterhood has to be put back together. No more "WE can't get along." It's for H.E.R. healing. There is a healing taking place. She has issues. We have issues. There is a divine connection that is mending H.E.R. life because you felt the pain first. Somethings were meant for you to help others heal.

Read Isaiah 55:8-9 for your H.E.R. Nugget

KEEP POUNDING!!

JOURNAL

Take time today to journal periods in your life that you didn't understand the why. It may be dates that were delayed, events that got postponed, a season of dryness, or a year of pain. Just begin to journal from the scripture. How were your thoughts of the pain different from what God had planned to strengthen you and develop you?

____

____

____

____

____

____

____

____

____

____

____

____

____

____

____

____

____

____

Day 26

YOU DON'T GET H.E.R.

You don't know how to understand H.E.R., so you don't know how to deal with H.E.R. You just don't get H.E.R. God didn't ask you to deal with H.E.R....God told you to love H.E.R. and God told you to treat H.E.R. as you would want to be treated. He never asked you for your opinion. He never asked for you to label H.E.R. either. Let's STOP destroying girl power. STOP mishandling sisterhood. STOP throwing away something that was supposed to be ENOUGH. You were not interested in greeting her like Mary greeted Elizabeth in the Bible. Mary was there for Elizabeth. They both needed one another. It is called supportive. When Mary heard her sister's voice, the Bible tells us her unborn child leaped; he moved inside of her. There has to be a **leaping** inside of H.E.R. when you show up. Whatever is developing inside of H.E.R. should leap at your encouraging voice and empowerment. She should trust you. She should feel secure with telling you H.E.R. story. Why isn't this happening with women? Why does she have to compete with you? Mary and Elizabeth both had favor with God. They were never jealous of one another. Just because you don't get her doesn't mean you can't be for her. We need to pray for the leaping. The leaping is a way of saying that the sisters shared love, concern, and wanted the best for one another. We must begin to pray for a lifelong bond with each other. There is a need for genuine support. Many of our sisters do not know how beautiful they are or how intelligent. Sisters all over the world have to stick together. This is our season, our year, and our moments to change the world together. You Rock, Sis! You are amazing! You are my sister! You are God sent! You are one of a kind! On the days that you don't feel accepted, smart, brilliant, wise, or worthy come back and read that many may not get you, but us sisters - WE GET YOU! God help H.E.R. to RELOAD our sisterhood. Amen.

Read Luke 1:41 for your H.E.R. Nugget

KEEP POUNDING!!

JOURNAL

As you navigate to this scripture in your Bible, get your pen out and journal your relationships with other women. Name the people who influence your purpose. Tell how you feel when you are around them & then discuss how some women really disturb your spirit. Write their names on the paper. Pray for them now. Call their names out and declare healing for them. Declare a healing on your heart if the reason they vex you is really you. We can't make ourselves always to be squeaky clean. They may need to know they are enough. They may need healing as much as you did. They also may need to be reloaded with trust, friendship, genuine love, respect, honor, and a softened heart. She may need to be simply EMPOWERED. Ask God to make what is being birthed inside of them leap as you show genuine support.

Day 27

BREAK UP

Lay your hands on yourself and tell the Lord, "I give you permission to pull me out of STUCK. I am ready to be stable in You. I am ready to go to the highest level. The next level You have for me. I have to be ready. I have to want better. I have come too far to quit now. It's my season. It's time to reap." God is looking for fruit bearers. Break up with depression. Break up with low self-esteem. Break up with dark places. Break up with circles and groups that aren't building you up or themselves. Don't allow that issue that you have no control over to cause you to delay your journey. Being stuck is behind you and you can see a fresh new future. Do you see more yet? Do you see yourself out? The sky is no longer the limit; your own thoughts are your LIMIT. You can be what you say you are. You can be what you see in your own heart. Today is your day. Read the words of the Bible and begin to feed your spirit, your confidence, your ability, and your recovery.

When you're on a journey of being ENOUGH, you can't be stuck. Today you will influence others. Today you will change the atmosphere everywhere your journey leads. You will no longer pick-up weight that doesn't belong to you. How does UNSTUCK feel? What does it mean in your life? In the book of Isaiah, around Chapter 43 it speaks to our journey, that God can do a new thing for us. Today tune your life and heart to all the new possibilities that can be yours. Your mind has to align with the new that God has for you. This begins to pull you out of being stuck. It's just like a tow truck. The tow truck pulls a stuck vehicle from a place where it wasn't able to move on its own. Those are the limits of tow truck. A wrecker can tow and make repairs. You have the same opportunity. You can rely on God to come to your rescue, tow you away from some negative circumstances, and repair your heart and your life. God is able to come to the place where no one else can pull you out of. He can fix your life!

KEEP POUNDING!!

JOURNAL

1. Read Proverbs 23:7 for your H.E.R. Nugget and memorize it.

____

____

____

____

____

2. Name one person you will encourage on H.E.R. journey.

____

____

____

____

____

3. Why do you think this woman was placed on your heart?

____

____

____

____

____

4. How can you impact H.E.R.?

____

____

____

____

____

____

5. How did being stuck weigh you down?

____

____

____

____

____

____

YOU ARE RELOADED FOR THIS ASSIGNMENT.

Day 28

WRESTLING MATCH

Why do you wrestle with the will that God has for your life? Stop the WRESLTING MATCH. Let go of your grip of control. God has to make all the calls from here on out. No longer do you have to wear yourself out fighting not to forgive, fighting not to let go, and fighting not to move on. You think of the pain and then begin to fight inwardly. When that happens, it's as though you want to keep all control. No longer will you be pinned down by thinking back to that wound, that soul tie, that mistake, that cycle, or that tender area that causes your eyes to fill up with tears. God wants to make you whole again in your thoughts and your heart. God is here to comfort you and pick you up to carry you daily.

God is here to listen and to release His strength to you. God is here to tell you to trust Him. God desires to sit and talk with you. God is here for your journey, the whole entire journey. God is standing by to listen to your side of the story. God wants to cover your heart. God wants to pour into you what no one can ever pour. God is changing your journey.

God is transforming your story. He understands and wants to address your pain. God is going with you. God can handle all the details, even the ones you don't necessarily want Him involved in. Give Him the bad relationship and turn the abuse over to Him. Surrender the adulterous spouse to God and remember that God wants the best for you with no exceptions. You are worth more. You are not here to lack. God is into YOU. God is your strong tower. God doesn't play when it comes to you. The wrestling match is 10, 9, 8, 7, 6, 5, 4, 3, 2, 1....OVER---that's a knockout. You are now on God's team. No more will you continue to wrestle. Raise your arms and praise God!

Read Genesis 32:24-34 for your H.E.R. Nugget

KEEP POUNDING!!

NEW THINGS

God doesn't want you to fret new things. We must forget those things which are behind us because our journey keeps us going forward. When seasons begin to change in our lives, we begin to change with the season. Can you do that on your journey? Can you make room for the newness of your soul, spirit, and mind? As our journey takes us through COVID 19 we witness people resisting the change. We see people disagreeing with the changes of socializing and traveling. This new way of living may not settle with what your normal has been. But in the midst of it all have you notice God himself doing new things in your life? It's time for new things but will you let God have the pain? Will you give God the person who left you? Well, you can't go forth if you are bringing all the baggage with you. Sis, if you bring all that with you on your H.E.R. journey it's too much weight for the flight. Do not let what you went through stop or hinder you from the new things. Do not let the turbulence scare you. It's part of the journey to your destiny. Get out of your thoughts. Get out of your feelings. Get out of the pity party. Choose to accept that it did not work out. But you are ready for the new! Take God's new boarding pass. Can I inform you that God is taking you to a new thing on this journey of healing and reloading? You will get through this and you don't have to go back to the past. Sis renew the passport! Sis get the window seat! Sis be happy right now! Sis do not look behind you. You can't leave a piece of you in the misery and have a piece of you moving on. This new thing is a blessing. This new season is what you prayed for. On this H.E.R. journey there is a change in the itinerary and a change in the seating assignment. Your name is being called to First Class and do not look back at the seat you moved from. You have a new seat. Receive this new thing and fly! Get the treatment you have waited for.

Read Isaiah 43:18-20 for your H.E.R. Nugget

KEEP POUNDING!!

Day 30

CONTAINERS

Guilt will not take up space in your mind. Your mind will be a CONTAINER of joy, love, peace, and positivity. You will not worry. Distractions will not control your thoughts. Anger won't take any valuable space. You will let go of all grudges. Today is your **no "offense" day.** You will not dwell on negativity and you will inventory what travels to your heart. Empty out today. Be filled with all the good things God says about you. Make room for a new perspective. It is time for you to empty your CONTAINER of life. God will overflow opportunities just for you. Let Him direct your steps. Let him push you in your journey. Worry (bye), Depression (bye), Bitterness (bye), Jealousy (bye), Doubt (get away from me).

Laughter (hello). Determination (hello). Strength (hello). Positivity (hurry, come on in). Regret (long gone). Self-pity (bye bye-it doesn't work anyway). Faith (welcome back!). Your container is now filled, prepared, and excited to start this day. You will not hold on to things that do not improve you. It is released. You must separate from negativity. Your container is durable! You have made room to be RELOADED. Do not punish yourself for things you didn't know before. This is a new container, and your life is living water, springing forth! This container holds success, laughter, a new glow, a positive attitude, and a totally new outlook. This container has purpose and puts a smile on your face. This container is filled with bold moves and a mindset of determination. This container has a destiny. This container is covered with God's love and promises. This container, Sis, is the portion of life you were beginning to doubt. This container is not filled with, "You can't make it." This container is packed with goodness and mercy shall follow you all the days of your life! All the days of your life. Of your journey. Of your legacy.

Read John 4:7-15 for your H.E.R. Nugget

KEEP POUNDING!!

JOURNAL

1. When the woman came to the well, she had a container/jug. The container was meant for her to use to draw water. What containers have you filled up with excuses and distractions on your journey?

____

____

____

____

____

2. Read verses 13 and 14. Name things that have gotten your attention off of your purpose. Write down and be honest in your writing about things that you were "thirsty" for but didn't lead you to purpose.

____

____

____

____

____

3. What things can you honestly say will soon be in your container because you will purposely include them on your new journey?

____

____

____

____

____

Day 31

TEMPTATION

Temptation = falling to a desire to do something wrong or unwise - displeasing God. If you yield to TEMPTATION, it could lead to sin and destruction in your life. When becoming H.E.R. you have to RESIST the enemy. You have to be ready to put the Word of God on anything the enemy deposits into your life. Fight the enemy by speaking the word. Say what God has said about your life. Speak up for the promises that are meant for you. God has interrupted your normally scheduled program so that you can fight back with praise. The enemy won't have your mind. God is bringing your mind out of depression. It is written you shall not live on bread alone but on EVERY WORD that comes from the mouth of God. Reinforce who you are in Christ. Remember you are the head and the bottom. Remember you are fearfully and wonderfully made. God gives you a way of escape. You can escape from temptation. The enemy looks for a window to climb through and door to push through. He looks for an ear to listen to him. He looks for a heart to overtake. He uses temptation to drag H.E.R. down. His mission is to steal your joy and kill your hope in God. He wants H.E.R. to have black eyes in her spirit and he wants to kill every dream you have. He desires to snatch your faith.

Don't come down from your great work. Don't stop your assignment. Temptation comes from Satan and your own fleshly desires. The enemy wants H.E.R. weak so he can kill, steal, and destroy everything on the path of your journey. But the devil will have no victory with you. He can't win a fixed fight. He can't defeat the word of God. He has no authority or rule over your spirit. You belong to God. God is taking ownership of the healed you. He adores you. He will hide you. God will protect you. God is your strong tower. He pulls you from the pit of temptation and confusion.

Read Matthew 4:4 for your H.E.R. Nugget

KEEP POUNDING!!

JOURNAL

1. Temptation comes to all people. How have you been tempted this week?

____

____

____

____

____

____

2. When temptation comes will you be able to talk back? Will you engage in your Bible to get words to declare over temptation?

____

____

____

____

____

____

3. Journal with scripture to support how you will resist the temptation. Use scripture over your mind and words.

____

____

____

____

____

____

Day 32

FIGHT SIS, FIGHT

It's time for you to win like a Believer! It's time for you to win like a woman. You have been in a battle, but you are not staying in the battle. Win the fight, Sis! This is the time on the journey when you look back and remember how God didn't let the enemy defeat Him. Jesus came to give you an abundant life! You are no longer going to give up on your family, your marriage, your children, your health, your dreams, your promises, your ministry, or your new life, without a fight. You will not go down easy this time. Go ahead and get the mamba mentality concerning your healing journey. You are on the move! You are dedicated to the work. Nothing can stop you. You have fresh oil on you! God has predestined your path. Keep on keeping on! Labor for this win! Do it when no one else see's what you see. You are a role model. You have fought some hard and tough fights. You have done things just like Noah in the Bible, without ever seeing anything like if before. Noah was building an ark because he was following instructions from God. This was a fight. Why? Because no one was willing to help or believe Noah. You will face fights just like Noah. But you keep building. You keep trusting that even if you look stupid, you do not quit. You have faced many battles. Keep conquering territory that was promised to you. Your assignment is to make it all the way to the other end of the journey! Sis, you are anointed to win for your family! Noah kept building and saved his family. You have to fight, Sis. Noah fought criticism. But God gave him favor. This journey of reloading is not going to be just given to you, but you do have favor. What is coming your way, you have never seen it like this. But Sis, the enemy doesn't want you to finish strong. Noah kept looking crazy until the day the rain came pouring down and he was safe in the ark-with his family. The enemy is trying hard to get what belongs to you. Keep this in your heart - the ark will get built. I can fight through negativity.

Read Joshua 11:1-9 for your H.E.R. Nugget

KEEP POUNDING!!

Day 33

WHAT IF

The mind can often times fill up with WHAT IF. The goal can be right there in your heart but then what if. That what if can cause depression, anxiety, suicidal thoughts, nervous breakdowns, loss of hope, disasters, negative thoughts, and it can turn H.E.R. into poor me. What if... the idea is not good enough? What if ...no one supports me? What if ...it doesn't work for me like it did for H.E.R.? What if...I never get married? What if...they don't hire me? What if...I tell the truth, and no one understands me? What if...that's not my purpose? What if he files for a divorce? What if.... I do have cancer? What if...the test comes back, and I have a lump in my breast? What if...I don't get chosen? What if...I fail? What if...my son doesn't get off of drugs? What if...I'm pregnant? What if...I just don't have what it takes? What if... they do not like me? What if...I'm not ENOUGH? What if ...I never get healed? What if... I don't know how to RELOAD...and start over? What if...I never lose the weight? What if... my plans do not work out? What if... I lose this time? What if... I do not get the second chance? Dump the

WHAT IF's? Let them go. You must not lean to your own understanding. It's time to TRUST GOD with all H.E.R. heart. Then you begin to understand that God didn't say those WHAT IF's to you, He has a God plan! Periodt! You will reach what God has for you to reach. The odds may be against you but press on! God is on your side! Possess it, Sis! There are no WHAT IF's to God being for you! God is with you always. So, you will not be defeated today and there are no ifs or ands about this. Hear from God and watch Him do what He says concerning you.

Read Proverbs 3:5 for your H.E.R. Nugget

KEEP POUNDING!!

Day 34

IT'S OKAY NOT TO BE OKAY

H.E.R. is often the superwoman, the one to get it all done, the supporter, the one who has your back, the one they call when they can't get their stuff to make sense and she pours all she has into EVERYBODY else ....and she finds herself NOT OK. She sits on the side of the bed and thinks what did I do for myself? How did the day go by so fast? Why do I feel so empty? Who am I to everyone in this WHOLE HOUSE? Do they care about me? Do I get a break? Should I run away? Who can I call to talk to? Oh Noooooo, she can't call anyone because SHE IS THE ONE with all the right answers. Right now, take a deep breath and write.......write how you are doing. Write about why it is okay for you to say, you are not okay sometimes.

KEEP POUNDING!!

JOURNAL

1. How do YOU feel right now? Why?

____

____

____

____

____

2. If someone asked you if you needed help would you respond with the truth?

____

____

____

____

____

3. Would you volunteer to go to speak with a therapist?

____

____

____

____

____

4. Do you understand you can't SAVE anyone else until you SAVE YOU?

____

____

____

____

____

5. What one person could you share your emotions with now?

____

____

____

____

____

Will you call them?

____

____

____

____

____

6. Today write what you can do for YOU today.

____

____

____

____

____

____

Bubble Bath_________   Short Walk______   Nap______

Relax and Do Nothing____

LET SOMEONE KNOW YOU ARE NOT OKAY AND IT'S FINALLY OKAY FOR YOU TO SAY SO. "HEY, I AM NOT OK. I DO NEED HELP. I DON'T HAVE TO HIDE IT ALL BEHIND THIS (MASK)."

Now dry your tears. Understand that you are fearfully and wonderfully made. This is healing. This is being enough to not be okay and express it. THIS IS BEING RELOADED ON OUR JOURNEY. You were not created to take the whole load. You were not created to tell lies about your emotions. You were not created to take on all of the world just because you are a mom, a wife, a single parent, an auntie, a friend, a leader, a mentor, or a sister. It takes honesty and knowing that you do not have to hold it all in ANYMORE.

Read Psalm 139:14 and write how it touched your heart.

____

____

____

____

____

____

Day 35

UNMASK

When you think of the (mask), the covering of H.E.R. face, so that she will not be contaminated with COVID, do you ever want to UNMASK? Is it time to uncover things you have kept covered in your heart? What does the mask represent for your spirit? For your soul? Unmasking in your spirit so that you can be free to be you with flaws and all. UNMASKING in your heart so that you can trust again. UNMASKING in your marriage with no filters to discuss issues that you hate the most. UNMASKING the junk in your mind that pops up when you think you are forgetting it ever happened. UNMASKING the things, you stack up and hoard in your mind. No more accumulating the past mistakes and failures. UNMASKING that generational curse that seems to go from you to your daughter and it just keeps moving in your family. It is time for you to UNMASK so that you can be RELOADED in your own mind, in your own future, and in your own dream before you leave this earth. UNMASKING the mess. What's the mess? It's the areas in your life that you cover up. You put a blockade there and you let no one in. As you go on your journey, discuss the UNMASKING. God is ready for the REAL you. UNMASK and come to HIM. Reveal your heart. Reveal to Him that sometimes you are scared to be JUST you. When you unmask before Christ, it's a time of refreshing, rebuilding, reorganizing, rebranding, restarting, rethinking, redirecting, repositioning, remembering, rebooting, restoring, redoing, remodeling, remobilizing, reconstructing, and accepting restoration for your brokenness. When you unmask, God sees you inwardly. When you unmask your heart, you can breathe again. Breathe again. Take a deep breath in your soul and live the life God has mapped out for you.

Read 1 Samuel 16:7 and 2 Corinthians 3:18 for your H.E.R. Nugget

KEEP POUNDING!!

Day 36

SWEET SPOT

What is the area of your heart that you KNOW God has purposely attached to you? It's your SWEET SPOT and you must know now....it will NOT leave your life. You work that area. You serve others in that area. You enjoy that area. You're wired in that area. You won't allow others to push you from it any longer. Often times you wake up and end your long day with that sweet spot in your mind. You and God will get it done. Ruth had a sweet spot of being faithful. Mary had a sweet spot of trusting God. She hid it in her heart when she was told she would have baby Jesus, even at a young age. Esther had a sweet spot of boldness. The time is now for you .... take hold of your passion and your purpose. Can you journal right here the things you can't shake? Write from your heart, from your passion; it's time to make it plain. Several times you have avoided that spot. You even tried to overlook that spot, but it is not just a normal spot. This is an area that is sensitive to God's direction. This area is a sweet spot for you because it doesn't take any effort; it is naturally how you are wired.

KEEP POUNDING!!

JOURNAL

1. What has God given you as a sweet spot? How will you share it with the world?

____

____

____

____

____

2. What ways have you tried to NOT follow through with the tug in your heart?

____

____

____

____

____

3. How do you feel when you can't operate in that sweet spot?

____

____

____

____

____

4. How are you rewarded, in your heart, when you are working in your sweet spot?

____

____

____

____

____

5. How will you stay committed to your passion?

____

____

____

____

____

6. How do you know that God inserted this in your heart?

____

____

____

____

____

7. Find a scripture in the Bible to help you pursue and stay consistent.

____

____

____

____

____

BOLD AFFIRMATION

Hug you! Affirm yourself! Declare positivity over you! Release the bitterness in your heart. Release the pressure. Allow healing to remain real. Let's remember that if Christ has worked things out, He will do it once again for you. You have to believe for good news and a good end. Bring your own good news of true healing. Announce to your heart that no more anger will reside in it. The enemy has no power over your joy. Be **BOLD!** Be fierce about your greatness! You are being RENEWED. You are being TRANSFORMED. This is the way H.E.R. has to start H.E.R. day.... being **BOLD** in YOUR mind, heart, and spirit. The boldness is necessary because you will not back down anymore when the enemy tries to direct your day. Do you want this **BOLDNESS** back in your life? ___Yes ___No

Prayerfully, you checked yes because that's the way we release and move forward. Are you ready to get rid of anger?
___Yes ___No (this question is important)
We do not want anger to guide our heart. So yes, be **BOLD** enough to admit what makes you angry?

Start you anger list. Name things/people that create anger inside of you.

1. ____

2. ____

3. ____

Get it all out now. Unpack. Keep writing.

____

____

____

____

____

____

Boldly pull it out of your own heart.

____

____

____

____

____

____

Read Ephesians 4:27 for your H.E.R. Nugget

KEEP POUNDING!!

Day 38

DEHYDRATION IN H.E.R. SOUL

The woman at the well can very well be a description of H.E.R. This woman had an encounter with Jesus but just moments before she was dehydrated in H.E.R soul. How do we know she was thirsty? She was doing life in a cycle. She was dry in her spirit and searched in all the wrong places for a quench. The Bible tells us that she came to draw water. Where have you been drawing your water? What jug are you bringing daily to your spot of rejection, embarrassment, or emptiness? When you are being filled with the love and compassion from Jesus, it brings forth a RELOADING to your spirit and life. There must be a time and place where you forget the jug you came to fill and begin to fill your life with the living water. Jesus told her all about H.E.R. self but He didn't leave H.E.R. in the state of mind that He met her in....she now had a voice. She was restored. She knew the truth about Jesus and herself. A conversion took place. Get your voice and go share with other women how Christ loves you, waited for you, and transformed your heart. This is our journey together. We build up. We share our testimony. We get the quench from Jesus that no one and nothing else can revive inside of us! The Living Water is the water for your spirit! It is a fountain you can live from!

Read John 4 for your H.E.R. Nugget

KEEP POUNDING!!

JOURNAL

1.   What's the jug (of doubt, rejection, cycles, embarrassment) that you will give up?

____

____

____

____

____

2.   What is the shame that Christ has healed you from?

____

____

____

____

____

3.   You no longer will thirst for the things of the world. Do you believe that if you start a relationship with Christ, He can forgive you? He can pour love into you.

____

____

____

____

____

NOT ALL BAD

Instructions....do you follow instructions? Do you make moves when you do not know when God is going to work things out? Does pressure make you move prematurely? What pressure pushes you to go ahead of the plans of God? Do you live by the word of God? Have you allowed that BAD situation to destroy your vision for your future? Your life has not been ALL BAD. You have more wins than losses. God has promised He will never leave you nor forsake you. Today can you just stand on the fact that God took care of you. God took care of the situation. God has provided more good days than bad days. You have to see your story differently. Think about it now. Did God show up in your sorrow? Did God show up when others showed out? Did He hold you when you were dealing with depression? Did God put you back together when you were broken into so many pieces? Didn't God come through for you? Change your story and tell about the goodness of God. Declare "that's not my story anymore." If you are honest. If you can be transparent, life is not all that bad. Become fluent in giving God glory! Be bold in saying what God has done for you! Speak what He did for you! Rise yourself up and command your mind, it's not all that bad. Talk to your own heart and say, "I haven't been broken all my life." Speak to your past and say, "I have a new story coming up now!" Pursue. Recover all. This is the season of obedience and you will win under pressure. I know you have failed before. I know you cried before. I know you thrown in the towel before. I know you quit before. You are on a journey now that went from losing to victorious! It hasn't been bad the whole time! Somethings you have believe and declare for yourself! You will be what God wants you to BECOME!

Read Psalm 23:1-6 for your H.E.R. Nugget

KEEP POUNDING!!

Day 40

H.E.R. AFFIRMATION

Some days are meant for H.E.R. to AFFIRM herself! It will no longer be hard for you to encourage yourself. Make today the day you go crazy about yourself!

The five **POWER P's** that PUSH H.E.R.

I have **PURPOSE** every single day of my life!

I have **PREPARED** for my new opportunities!

I have **POSITIONED** myself to prosper!

I have **PLANS** that can NOT be stopped!

I have **PRAYED** to God! And He answers!!!

I will ____

I can ____

I have ____

I won't ____

You are able to keep going. PRESS, PUSH, PROPEL.......

Learn to be your best supporter. Learn to say power words over your mind, your health, your journey, and your family. No matter what life brings your way, take it, and create a place where YOU bring your own affirmation. God can change my day, my story, and my journey.

List several words that you no longer want to describe you. Mark out the negative words after you write them here:

______________,_____________________________,___________________

_________,_______________________,_________________________________,_____

Read Proverbs 18:4 for your H.E.R. Nugget

KEEP POUNDING!!

DAY OF DESIRES

The Bible says that God will give H.E.R. the desires of H.E.R. heart. (that's you)

God, I desire_________________________________because

____

God, I desire_________________________________because

____

God, I desire_________________________________because

____

God, I desire_________________________________because

____

God, I desire_________________________________because

____

My family desires______________________________because

____

I will continue to depend and lean on you, God. You now have all my desires. You have all my family desires. I thank You for giving them to me in Your perfect timing. I won't rush them because I know You have it all planned out for me. Throughout the day begin to say: **I will delight myself in the Lord and He will give me the DESIRES of my heart.**

Read Psalm 37:4 for your H.E.R. Nugget

KEEP POUNDING!!

<h1 style="text-align:center">Day 42</h1>

DEEP INSIDE THE FISH

God's grace is sufficient. Those words should find a place in your heart. There is no need to run from what God has called you to do. There is no time to be wasted going the opposite direction. Time is valuable and can't be given back. There is no time to do it your own way. Do you have your very own agenda? Think of times when you knew you should have surrendered to God. Lessons learned can also push you to where you need to be. He wants to lead you. Even in the belly of the big fish Jonah was still cared for and loved by God. Has God told you something important to do? Have you ran? Are you running today? Why? Sometimes running is from fear. Sometimes running is because of distractions. Sometimes running keeps you from reliving certain portions of your journey. Sometimes running keeps you from seeing all you are actually capable of completing. Running can take place as a reaction to realizing you have an assignment that is bigger than you. Running can also take you further and further away from the truth. Running can distance you from the voice of God.

How long does it take you to submit? How long does it take you to pray? How long does it take you to obey? Obedience is crucial. No longer will you be the one who runs from God's perfect plan. Once you study Jonah's story, you will discover that God can take you out of the comfy places in your life and focus in on His plans for you. You can't run away because God is ahead of you. The Bible says that God had prepared the belly of the whale just for Jonah. He knows which way you are going and how deep you will go. Do not attempt to flee. A significant spiritual release is near, in your obedience it will be revealed.

Read Jonah 1:1-17 for your H.E.R. Nugget

KEEP POUNDING!!

Day 43

HAVE FAITH

During this journey that you are on, you will need to have faith. I know you have heard people say things like, where is your incredible faith? Or do you have big faith? Big faith is not required, nor the faith Big Mama had. The Bible says, we just have to have "faith" to please God, with no quantity attached to it. The Bible nails it even further when it tells us to have a mustard seed faith. A mustard seed is very tiny. If you have little faith, you can begin to say words that build. When you hear your own words of faith, you can hear what is going on within you. Let faith come out of your mouth. You do not have to be anxious, depressed, or suicidal about situations. God saw the faith of the woman washing his feet, Ruth, Queen Esther, and Mary the mother of baby Jesus. Block out what faith looks like to people. Your faith is seen in your heart by God. Apply your faith and witness movement. When you speak faith, then you S.O.A.R higher. As you use your faith, God puts the wind above your wings so you can accelerate. Reshape, restart, and reimagine your journey with faith sealing the deal. This faith can move what was pinning you down. Start now using your little faith in BIG ways. You won't be able to see it all. You won't be able to feel the tangible, but you still have faith. See, the faith you have now is you trusting and having confidence. You are no longer skeptical on this journey. You have come this far and there is no looking back.

Read Matthew 17:20 (NIV version) and Hebrews 11:6 for your H.E.R. Nugget

KEEP POUNDING!!

Day 44

USE THE WORD

The Bible is available; but if the word of God is not applied there will not be a transformation. Do you desire a real encounter with God? This is one of the steps, desiring to understand the biblical principles. There is a great need to turn the word of God on in your everyday life. Do you understand how to use it? On this journey it is necessary for the word of God to be hidden in your heart. That means try to get alone and read to feed your soul. When you study the Bible, study it to get nourishment. Study to get answers. Study the word so you can live! The word will build you up with strength. The word of God is your GPS and your spiritual direction. The Word commands your journey. The Word fills you with Hope. The Word of God gives you momentum. The Word of God corrects you. The Word of God tells you what you need to hear. The Word of God helps you. The Word wants you to win. Today you will have clarity and confidence that you can also hear from God. You no longer have to wait on others to feed you this truth. You will have clarity, you will have a prayer life, and you will have the presence of God working in your life as you open your Bible. Begin to visualize yourself engaging and hearing God's voice in the scripture. Ask yourself questions: What does this mean for my life? How can I do what the word is saying to my heart? Do I believe it for me? Now is your opportunity to be stable and have a peace of mind as you lean on the scriptures you read (daily). Can you say this: **"I want to hear God's voice for myself today and every day of my life."** This has to be your personal commitment.

Read Psalm 119:11 for your H.E.R. Nugget

KEEP POUNDING!!

Day 45

THAT VERY THING

Get ready! Get set! Let's go! Get rolling with your mind steady on Jesus! You need a daily charge! A daily dose! That Very Thing... is called PRAISE!! PRAISE can get you started! Start a day of "Let it go." Start a day of Rejoicing! Somethings just have to be released. Why not let a Praise be released into your home! Somethings you have to set your mind to drop. Some people you have to be left in the past. Some relationships will have to be resigned. There is purpose in your pain. But that very thing is God has done great things for you! So why not Bless the Lord right now? Yes, it will be the way you will be freed! See, there will be no more shame. Did you do it? Yes, you did...but year after year you are beating yourself up because of it. Turn up for Christ. Give Him a Shout! He deserves all you have today. The very thing that is missing from your morning is giving God some glory! No longer, Sis, can you allow this to eat at your heart, eat at your spirit and eat at your self-worth. Call on the name of the Lord! He is worthy to be praised! That very thing that God wants most from you is your surrender. He wants to hear your heart of gratitude. Let him hear it. Let him feel your faith. Bless God! No, you are not where you planned to be by now. But lose yourself in him. His name can heal. His name can save. His name can deliver. Can you prepare your heart to receive this breakthrough? Dry those tears. Wipe your face. Roll up your spiritual sleeves and say, "I have had enough." And then within your heart, cry out, "Lord transform my life. I want to get over the rejection, the divorce, the abandonment, and the loneliness. Trust in the Lord. Let him direct you path. This is your time now for transformation. You are the apple of God's eye. God wants you whole. God desires for His daughter to allow Him to reload your thoughts, reload your mouth, and reload your strength and sanity. He's got you. Go ahead and give God PRAISE. Keep the Faith!

Read Psalm 95:1-11 for your H.E.R. Nugget

KEEP POUNDING!!

Day 46

DROPPED ON ACCIDENT

Mephibosheth in the Bible was the son of Jonathan. At an incredibly young age he was dropped on accident by the person that was to be taking care of him. This was not done to him on purpose. His nurse had taken him and was running due to a hostile situation that was taking place and Mephibosheth was dropped. He became lame (crippled) in both of his feet. On your journey, some things and actions done to you were not intentional. Everyone that hurt you did not do this on purpose. Some people wanted to help and encourage but their efforts went the wrong way. You may have felt let down by people or a person that you loved and trusted. Things happen in real life that can't be reversed. How has this crippled the way you communicate with others? Do you feel like you were dropped? Do you ever feel hopeless? How has the drop that took place in your younger life made you unable to move ahead with certain people? Do you have an area on your journey that can be tender to talk about? God has not forgotten you. Years later, Mephibosheth was blessed. God remembered him. He was taken out of that dark place. Can God take you from your Mephibosheth situation? Did that death due to COVID-19 put you in a crippled place? Did the father of your child disappoint you? Did something very painful cripple your ability to love again? Did that painful relationship, addiction, and/or suffering keep you motionless? Some of us were dropped but it was in the midst of our mothers running from an abusive relationship or her trying to give us a better life. It's nothing that was done on purpose... but it still hurt. It was still a dark place. Accidently being hurt can still affect your life-your journey. Trauma refers to a deeply distressing experience. Lord, that's me. I know you are about to shift my journey and get me healed of the trauma.

Read 2 Samuel 4:4 and 2 Samuel 9:3-12 for your H.E.R. Nugget

KEEP POUNDING!!

Day 47

STAY WOKE

There is a point on this journey that we have to watch how we are living. As we watch, we do not allow the enemy to just come and take up space in our thoughts, heart, or our home. When we guard our belongings, it won't be easy for distractions. It's time to activate our prayer time and then keep praying without backing down on our talks with Jesus. It will take consistency. Keep praying and keep believing. When you watch it means you are staying in a position of seeking God. As you seek God, you continue to zoom in on what takes place in your circles, your home, your thoughts, and your emotions. Often times we get sleepy or weary at times when we should stay woke. There will come times when we have to eliminate or take out the spiritual attacks. Understand that you have to keep your mind steady, sober, and focused on God. Jesus desires for his daughters to keep our hearts and eyes wide open spiritually. Bottom line is we CANNOT stop PRAYING. Your prayers are beating your flesh into submission through agreeing with the word of God. The more you watch. The more you guard, you will be intentional about staying woke. Stay woke so you can defeat the enemy. Stay woke so you can win. Stay woke so you won't stay in cycles. There are times like the times we are all facing now that your position is in your prayer closet, the place where you can go in and close the door so you can pour out your soul to God. Being reloaded on our journey is us praying for one another. We can't pray for one another if we do not pray for ourselves daily. The daily prayer builds us up to have discernment for our sisters, our families, and our future. This place of prayer builds our strength and keeps our peace. As you transform into H.E.R. (healed, enough & reloaded) you must stay woke. Don't sleep on your purpose, your destination, nor your responsibility of prayer. Stay woke.

Read Matthew 26:36-40 for your H.E.R. Nugget

KEEP POUNDING!!

Day 48

CRA- CRA- CRAZY

You are still committed. You are still praising God. You are still obeying. You are still seeking to grow. You are still glorifying God. You are still telling about how good God is. You are still envisioning better. All the time you are (still) the people around you think you are crazy. See some folks will not get it. Some folks won't get why in the midst of a crisis, you are still crazy about pleasing God. So, despite how things seem to be out of control, you are (still) trusting God. You are still being faithful, looking crazy. You are still spending time in your word, looks crazy. By now on your healing journey, you look cra- cra- crazy to some people. You are still tithing but can't go to the church building. You are still attending Bible Study virtually, that looks super crazy. You are still staying on TRACK. You are still leaning on God. You are still walking around with joy. Even though you do not know exactly what tomorrow may look like, you still continue to rely on the promises of God. If you read Luke 1:26-38, you will see that Mary was a young girl when told that she would be pregnant with baby Jesus. Mary had to go around the community, people saw her trusting God. She hid in her heart what was promised to her. She was told she found favor with God. How did being pregnant without laying down with a man look like favor? This young Mary was told that the spirit will come upon you and the power of the Highest will overshadow you. Still Mary trusted God. There will be times on your H.E.R. journey where your belief, trust, and honoring God's word will make you look crazy. What is it that God has placed inside of you that seems insane? What has God purposed you to carry that seems bananas to them? What has God spoken to your heart that you know will make you look like the fool of the month? Well, if God has downloaded and purposed in you things that blow your mind it's because it will happen.

Read Luke 1:26-38 for your H.E.R. Nugget

KEEP POUNDING!!

Day 49

THE WORST IS OVER

Sometimes you can't network yourself out. Sometimes your kindness can't get you out. Sometimes your knowledge can't get you out. Sometimes your money can't get you out. Sometimes your lie can't get you out. Sometimes your parents can't get you out. Sometimes your best friend can't get you out. Nobody and nothing but God can get you out of some things. The relationship seems like it will never get restored. The dream looks so far out. The health report starts looking final. This is when you have to totally trust in God. There is a time in your life when you have to come to terms that only God can get you out of this one. Learn to depend on God like never before. Living in the times we are living in now; your smartness won't work. Leaning to your own understanding won't work. Surrendering to God works. It works because He can move in the plans He has for you. Allow God to order your steps. The worst is over on your journey. There are brighter days now. God continues to rescue an unlimited amount of times. He loves to swoop down and rescue you. Can you start declaring and praising God today just because you believe things are coming together for you? You have been in this place long enough and it has been a struggle. The struggle is ending. Matter of fact, the struggle is over. The Rescuer is here once again. Sometimes the worst times develop a long-lasting relationship with God. The devil meant bad to consume you, but God has turned it all around for your good. When you feel like giving up can I suggest you try Jesus? Trying Jesus means that you will pray. It means that you will declare that God was with you the entire journey. Those vulnerable moments will not destroy you, they will develop the "inner you".

KEEP POUNDING!!

JOURNAL

1. How will you begin to trust God?

____

____

____

____

____

____

2. Journal some things that you will begin to give to God.

____

____

____

____

____

____

Day 50

GIRL LIVE YA LIFE

Her victory walk was iconic on November 7, 2020. The lyrics ringing loud and clear from Mary J. Blige's hit song "Work That." It brought cries of joy to many women. Women who are H.E.R. She walked for us. She stood for us. We could feel HER words in our hearts no matter what our political affiliation was.

Mary J. Blige, later in an interview stated, "she didn't see that coming" when the song was used for our Vice President Elect Kamala Harris during her victory walk. Mary also said while being interview that "Kamala Harris made it be a part of her history." The song written by Mary J. was used on such a memorable day in our history, Vice President Elect Kamala Harris' first speech to the nation on an evening that changed the world for women. She shared in her speech "I may be the first but won't be the last." Ladies, there is so much more ahead for us. Through this devotion my prayer is that we will see that God has a purpose already written out concerning us.

Why did I end with this? Because you and I are women who through the strength of God can do anything. We are making history. We are better together. We are on our journey.

Read Philippians 4:13 for your H.E.R. Nugget

KEEP POUNDING!!

JOURNAL

1. What inspired you through Vice President Elect Kamala Harris' victory?

____

____

____

____

____

____

2. How did you see your dreams being more realistic on November 7th, 2020?

____

____

____

____

____

____

3. Will you continue to pound even when things seem difficult?

____

____

____

____

____

____

4. Do you believe that through God you can do amazing things?

____

____

____

____

____

____

5. What's next on your H.E.R. Journey?

____

____

____

____

____

____

"Purpose is an essential element of you. It is the reason you're on the planet at this particular time in history. Your very existence wrapped up in the things you're here to fulfill......the struggles along the way are only meant to shape you for your purpose."

Chadwick Boseman

#42